Matched To His Tiger

Van Cole

Published by Van Cole, 2023.

This is a work of fiction. Similarities to real people, places, or events are entirely coincidental.

MATCHED TO HIS TIGER

First edition. May 12, 2023.

Copyright © 2023 Van Cole.

ISBN: 979-8223253754

Written by Van Cole.

Table of Contents

Matched To His Tiger
Gay Paranormal MPREG Romance

By: Van Cole

Foreword

Lance and Ewan live on totally opposite ends of the same spectrum.

Lance, having lived as the High Alpha of a secret tiger shifter Streak his entire life, is itching to get out and experience the world beyond the boundaries of the forest in which he lives. At night he gazes down into the glittering lights of the city, and wonders what it would be like to leave everything he knows behind, and indulge his curiosity among the very beings who threaten his people's existence.

Ewan, meanwhile, finds himself cooped up in an office at all hours, his life a stuffy and miserable one. A tiger shifter himself, he was adopted by a human family when he was only a child, and has never really felt he had much of a place in the world in which he lives. He wonders whether there could possibly be others out there who are like them, or whether he'll be forced to spend the rest of his life in hiding, denying his true self.

It seems like fate, then, when the two men's paths happen to cross at a bar one evening, and they spend the night together in the rapturous throes of ecstasy, revealing their true selves in a way that they've seldom done to anyone else around them.

Could this be true love at first sight?

Or will the rolling of their paths in opposite directions doom their relationship before it's even had the chance to begin?

Matched To His Tiger

Matched To His Tiger

Chapter 1

The night was still. The air cool and motionless.

The forest was silent, save for the nearly imperceptible hum of insect life above the deafening emptiness.

Then, out of nowhere-

A sudden flash of movement.

Small woodland creatures scrambled out of the way as the beast came trundling toward them like a rocket- a strange, exotic creature which had no place in an area of the world such as this, but which they knew all the same, as if by instinct, must surely mean them harm.

They pushed themselves into burrows and trembled for their lives, but the massive beast paid them no mind.

It ran on past, taking no notice whatsoever of the life now cowering beneath its expansive footsteps. Its claws dug into the soil of the undergrowth, tearing up showers of dirt with every tremendous leap, dipping and twisting around the trunks of trees, bobbing and weaving beneath low branches, and navigating the whole of the forest with expert precision.

This was the beast's home after all- the only home it had ever known.

And the very same home it was now contemplating leaving behind...

It ran without any clear goal apparent in its mind, aside from the obvious burning away of energy. The need to escape, to free itself from the confines of its own thoughts. Its mighty flanks heaved from the effort of its running, its tail whipped across the leaves as it went, and its black stripes seemed to strobe in the shadows beneath the pale light of the moon, light, dark, light, dark, light, dark.

A fully grown tiger, erupting through the darkness as though on some sort of rampage, its ears lowered to its head, its eyes narrowed on the horizon as it ran.

It was just like any other night, it thought.

It might take an hour or two, or three or four, but eventually it would tire itself out. It would feel the rush of adrenaline, the oneness with the natural world which surrounded it. These would be enough to sustain it, and to remind it of all that it had to be thankful for in life- as well as all that it had to lose.

Yet, at the same time, none of these things was coming to it with particular ease.

The cat could feel the pressure of its desires growing stronger and stronger as its speed intensified. It was like trying to outrun a storm, and finding yourself inundated no matter how fast you were capable of going.

The longer it ran, the more its only thought was of escape.

Like these vast, expansive woods represented no kind of freedom at all, but a prison.

Like the cat itself had spent its entire lifetime behind the bars of a cage like some zoo animal, instead of as the powerful alpha male that he truly was, the strongest and most respected individual among a Streak of his own kind.

But no amount of forward momentum, of trying to convince himself that what he had was what he truly wanted, could possibly change the facts of the matter...

And so he just kept running.

He ran and ran, rising up along a hillside toward a spot where he often went when he felt like this. A place where he could look down onto the whole of his territory, and truly feel like the king that he was. The rock glowed softly in the illumination of the full moon above, and seeing it rise into view spurred him into a still greater pace, his longing to be relieved of this angst becoming nearly unbearable.

He made his ascent to the very top of the rock, his claws chipping away at the stone as he mounted his position. Then, shoving his chest forward, craning his head back, and opening his jaws as wide as they could possibly go, he let out a deep, long, mighty roar.

"ROOOOOOOOOWWWWWWWWWWWW!"

The sound boomed out into the night, so loud as it shimmied through the treetops that several sleeping birds were disturbed from their nests, and went fluttering off in fear.

It was an incredible feeling, and so he did it again, then a third time, his roars gradually diminishing in enthusiasm until finally he just stood there, panting, his eyes shifting from side to side as he gazed at his surroundings.

He surveyed the tops of the trees, and felt, for a fleeting moment, exactly how he'd been longing to feel.

Powerful.

In control.

Holding dominion over-

Over what?

Trees...

Just trees.

He let out a little snarl of contempt at this, and slightly lowered his head.

He looked around briefly, as though searching for some sign of something, anything, that might make him feel one iota better about his situation.

He found nothing, and realized that he'd known that this would be the case before he even started looking.

The tiger stood there panting, his whiskers twitching slightly, his heart rate steadily returning to normal.

Then he rose, and stood up onto his haunches.

His body began to shrink.

The luscious golden fur that covered every inch of him receded into his flesh, the stripes disappearing, save for a few bands of jet black tattoos that corresponded to them across his back, chest, shoulders, and thighs. His feline body gave way to a rugged, chiseled physique, entirely human, and entirely masculine. His washboard abs heaved with exertion as he

strained to catch his breath, and the determination in his eyes gradually fell to sadness.

He stared off into the distance for as long as he could stand it, determined to find something that might provide him with the hope he'd been looking for.

Then he turned his head, and stared off in the opposite direction, toward the sole beacon of hope that had been sustaining him, for nearly as long as he could remember.

The twinkling white bulbs of the city in the distance, competing with the curtain of starlight overhead...

They called to him, as they always did.

They made promises to him, promises that became harder and harder for him to resist with each new visit.

He gritted his teeth, and took in a deep breath.

He let his mind wander down into those busy, illuminated streets, projecting himself in a world that he'd never known before, except within his fantasies.

Stop it... Just stop it Lance, he chided himself, feeling like he was on the verge of something dangerous. Getting closer and closer to it with every new visit. Drawing so close to the edge, so close to leaving everything behind, edging toward the oblivion of his own destruction.

How much further would he go?

How much further could he go, before he went too far?

He could see himself now, plummeting over the edge, cascading through freefall without any kind of hope of recovering himself again.

It made his bones rattle in his body. Made his chest heave wildly.

And yet none of it stopped him from putting a single foot forward, sliding it across the stony ground, as though to at last make the move he'd been contemplating for so many nights on end.

He held it there, his flat sole stretched out across the ground, waiting, waiting, as though for some manner of signal.

And that was when it came...

"Do it," said a deep, almost eerily steady voice in his ear.

He promptly drew his foot back, as if by doing so fast enough he might conceal the fact that he'd even been considering such a departure. He spun around on his heel, away from the glittering lights of the city, and stared instead into the dark eyes, the two black voids in the center of a malevolent face

"Ulric..." he snarled at the man. Next to himself, Ulric was the most powerful alpha male in his Streak. He'd long held a grudge that Lance himself had been granted a position so much higher than his own despite the negligible differences in their abilities. Whether it was Lance's familial connections that led to his ascent to high alpha, or simply the fact that he'd never managed to overtake his position, the man standing before him had never had any great qualms about keeping his unhappy feelings for the Streak leader known.

"Go on," Ulric continued, waving a casual hand at the city in the distance. "We both know it's what you want. Leave your people behind. Abandon us. Like the weak and ineffectual leader that you are..."

Lance spat on the ground.

"Go to hell," he said. "I came up here to clear my head, that's all..."

Ulric laughed at this, and shook his head.

"I can see it in your eyes," he said matter of factly. "Even facing away from the lights of the city, you're staring so far into the distance. Like you really aren't here at all... Do you really think our people deserve a man like you leading us? A man whose heart is so clearly elsewhere? Don't you think we have enough problems as it is, without our high alpha pining to join the very human filth who threaten our survival?"

Lance's blood was starting to boil. His hands curled into fists, his heart beat violently in his chest. He had a vicious desire to rear back and punch Ulric's teeth in- possibly because, more than anything, he knew that there was considerable truth to what he was saying, even if it was the last thing he would admit to himself in a million years.

Instead, as though he might provoke violence from him as an excuse to retaliate, he stepped across the cliff to where Ulric stood, widening his shoulders as far as he could, and pressing his bare chest up against him, daring him to strike.

"If you have a problem with me," he said, "All you need to do is say so. It'll be entirely too easy for the two of us to settle things if that's the case..."

Ulric's expression hardened for a moment. His eyes glistened black, and for a second it appeared entirely likely that he might just take the bait, and give Lance the very fight he was now itching for.

But then he just smiled.

He drew his body back just enough to lift up a hand between the two of them. He stretched a hand out against the center of Lance's chest, and pressed him gently back away from them- doing so just effortlessly enough to piss Lance off even further.

Lance stepped back, his nostrils flaring, and once a short distance separated the two men Ulric lowered his hand again, giving him a sickening smile. He shook his head.

"I'll leave you to your rumination," he said, turning away, and making for the slope he'd ascended to get here. Once he'd made it to its edge he craned his neck around, and added with a sneer, "I just think it would be easier if you stopped pretending you had anyone fooled. Not even yourself..."

"Thank you for your input," said Lance.

Ulric grinned at him, then turned back to face the darkness. He leapt forward, and his body vanished on the spot, the massive striped form of a fully grown tiger receding into shadow, and rustling through the undergrowth for a short time until finally he was altogether gone.

Lance took a deep, shuddering breath.

Tears were in the corners of his eyes.

He hated Ulric so much in that moment, almost as much as he hated himself.

How could he even consider it? Turning his back on the people who needed him... Abandoning the position of the high alpha, and in doing so likely abdicating his role to such a power-hungry lowlife as Ulric, who would almost certainly take over...

And yet, at the same time-

How could he not?

How could he live his entire life enshrined in these worlds? Trapped by his primitive society and their primitive customs? Wandering toward extinction as their numbers dwindled, forced to live as nomads while a whole world beyond the boundaries of the forest awaited them?

How could he not allow himself to experience the life that the human world had to offer? How could he live the rest of his life never knowing all that he was missing out on, and only imagining the many fruits that living freely dangled in front of him?

How much longer could he keep pretending that this was the only life he was meant for?

He took another deep breath, holding it for almost a minute. Then he exhaled, and stepped back toward the slope. Returning in the direction he'd come from, thinking that his fantasy would still be there the following night. And the night after that. And the night after that.

Indefinitely...

The city, after all, wasn't going anywhere.

He disappeared into shadow as Ulric had done. And for almost another minute all was silent. All was still. The fingers of a cool breeze caressed the top of the cliff, and nothing more.

And then, in a flash of movement, the lumbering orange cat came shooting back up along the slope, racing as fast as he could across the forest's apex, up one side of the mountain and then immediately down along the other.

He ran with all his might in the direction of the city, his muscles tearing as he shot across the ground, his ears ringing, determined as he was to make it there before he had the opportunity to change his mind.

Finally, he decided, it was time for a decision to be made...

Chapter 2

The little silver balls of Newton's cradle clacked back and forth beneath the single fluorescent light still on over Ewan's cubicle. He sat hunched over with his fingers combed through mussed up hair, his eyes flickering back and forth as he watched the two little globes on either end swinging out, tapping on the central spheres without seeming to affect them at all.

He felt hypnotized, unable to look away.

Anything to take his mind off the mountains of paperwork still towering over him, not to mention the endless potential of the life he felt certain he was throwing away.

He leaned back in his desk chair and sighed. He closed his eyes and they burned as he did so, but he kept them shut for a long time anyway, trying to clear his head.

This isn't the life I'm supposed to be living, he told himself. It never was... It never will be... So why do I keep trying to convince myself that it is?

He sat down his pen and tried to flex the cramps out of his hand, shaking it briskly through the air. He could feel the claws beneath his fingertips, aching to get out. Could feel his jaws prickling, the animal version of himself begging to be free.

And yet he knew that that could never happen... Knew that was a part of him that could never be free, so long as he lived, at the risk of throwing everything away.

As though he really had that much worth holding onto so tightly in the first place...

He turned back to his work and stared at it for so long that his throat began to hurt. Then, finally, he gave up on getting any more done for the night, his temples throbbing, his muscles aching.

He really needed a drink...

He threw down his pen, and didn't even bother cleaning up his workstation.

In a few hours everything would still be there waiting for him, right where he'd left it.

He packed together his belongings, switched off his desk lamp, and made his way toward the exit.

"Goodnight Albert," he called with a wave of his hand to the custodian in the hallway, who was busy noisily waxing the floor as he made his way past. Albert absently lifted up a hand and waved at him, and Ewan carried on.

He felt like he and Albert were starting to become far too acquainted with one another these days...

———

Soon Ewan found himself hunched over at the bar, his body in very much the same position it had been in at his desk. Hand on his head. Shoulders slumped forward. His eyes staring a thousand yards into the distance.

At least now he had a drink in his hands- not to mention in his bloodstream. It didn't take the feeling away, though. Just sort of spread it out, made it feel hazy and indistinct as it spread through his body. Like he couldn't actually lay a hand on any one of his individual problems, but it just sort of engulfed him, like an aura of some kind.

He simply couldn't escape the certainty that this wasn't the life he'd been meant for.

That he'd been born in the wrong place, under the wrong circumstances for someone like him.

Or that maybe, it was just himself that was the problem.

Maybe a person like him could never really belong anywhere...

He continued to sip slowly at his drink, trying his best to pace himself. Part of him felt like getting wasted, but another, more practical part of him didn't want to face coming into work with a hangover the next morning.

God, I can't even get drunk right, he thought, and almost had to laugh himself.

What he hadn't anticipated, with his hair a mess, his work clothes askew across his broad frame, and his face feeling like it might melt away from his skull at any given moment, was for any man in this place to show even the remotest interest in him, even though the idea of going home with someone felt like just the medicine he needed right now to treat what was ailing him.

He was surprised then, when he glanced up to see a pair of eyes gazing down at him across the bar.

It caught him off-guard, and he nearly choked on his drink, but managed to keep from spitting it back out into his glass with a supreme effort. He swallowed, then tried to look up at him from his periphery, not wanting to be too obvious about it.

He hadn't just been imagining it...

The man was indeed looking over at him- and he was a damn fine looking man at that...

His skin looked tan, almost caramelized in the dim light of the bar. He had jet black hair and, looked at indirectly at least, eyes that seemed to glow an almost neon yellow, like the eyes of a cat. Ewan felt his neck getting hot, his balls tightening up into his body, and a not unpleasant burn running along the neck of his manhood, causing a hot lengthening down along the leg of his pants.

He took a deep breath, trying to control himself.

It seemed almost too good to be true...

He'd always been a little bit shy about this sort of thing. Dating, in general. He wasn't the most openly gay man around, and he didn't think he necessarily seemed all that "on the market" to men who might be interested in him- much less, to men such as the one he now thought was staring at him.

It was by design, to a degree. He'd always been so afraid of losing control, letting his life slip away from him if he dared surrender himself to anyone too fully. It wasn't exactly the biggest secret in his life, but it was still something he held close to his chest these days, feeling as he did like he needed to really trust someone before he could indulge such intimacies as the full truth about himself.

He continued to look down at his glass, sipping on it until nothing but the ice cubes remained at the very bottom. He stared at the little clear mountain of ice for a moment, then forced himself to bravely glance all the way up, and look his potential predator directly in the eyes for the first time.

He was still staring over at him.

Still gazing at him with his sharp eyes, which were actually green now that he got a clear look at them, but which still seemed to glow unnaturally at him. They were like marbles, or something, glistening through the darkness.

On top of his masculine perfection, his nostrils were flaring softly in his direction. It was sexy as hell, making Ewan feel even more like prey than he already did.

He still wasn't sure about all of this- whether he could let his guard down for a night of carefree ecstasy, as he was now feeling so viciously tempted to do.

Now though, he discovered that he was already playing the man's game.

He couldn't pull his eyes away, but found himself staring over at him, his own nostrils flaring back at him, picking up on something that wasn't quite typical.

There was a scent about him... Something he recognized, but which he couldn't exactly place.

He'd never actually smelled it on anyone before...

Whatever it was, though, it felt like sheer, animal lust. Throbbing through his veins, making his jaw quiver, his skin heat up. A wave of panic lurched through his stomach, and he had a desperate urge to get up right there on the spot and run, get as far away from there, from that man looking over at him, as he possibly could.

But God, now his erection was practically tearing through his pants, keeping him glued to his seat for fear of being seen. It was like the man had employed it as a weapon against him, knowing exactly how to incapacitate him, and how best to use the fact to his advantage.

Stay calm... Just stay calm, he tried to tell himself.

He looked away from him again, hoping that he could settle himself down long enough to figure this out.

But then, there he was.

Standing from his barstool.

Gliding over in his direction, his eyes not moving from him.

Taking a seat beside him.

"Evening," he said, a little smile on his face.

Ewan looked up at him, barely able to meet his gaze directly at first. He could feel his face glowing red at him, and could barely keep his eyes open through the sweat rolling down along his skin in thick, hot rivulets. Once he managed to meet his gaze, however, he found himself transfixed, unable to look away.

His mouth hung open a little bit, and he managed with great effort to form words around the dryness on his tongue.

"Hey," he said, smiling feebly at him. This only made the man's grin spread further.

"You alone?" he asked.

"Not anymore," said Ewan, and saying it sent a tingle of sensation across his cheeks. God, he thought, where the hell did that come from? He felt like a woman or something...

The man laughed though, and Ewan did too, shaking his head.

"Sorry," he said, "I think I've had too much to drink..."

"Cheers to that," said the man, lifting his own glass to him. "One more round shouldn't hurt anything then, do you think? On me?"

Ewan opened his mouth, closed it, and then nodded at him.

The man tapped on the bar to get the bartender's attention.

"Hey, could we get another round over here?"

The man behind the bar sat out two more glasses, filled them, and slid them over to the men. They clinked them together, and drank.

"Thanks," said Ewan, gasping slightly as he pulled the tumbler from his lips. "I think I did need that..."

The man laughed.

"You looked a little bit like you might have..."

Ewan stared absently at him for a moment. He was wearing a super tight t-shirt, the black fabric conforming to a muscular physique underneath that did little to help with the problem of his arousal. He also noticed, just below his sleeves, a series of black striped tattoos on both arms, stopping just above his elbows.

This stirred something deep inside his chest.

It couldn't be... Could it?

No, he must just be imagining it... Seeing what he wanted to see...

Plenty of people must have tattoos that were exactly like that, after all. Nothing unusual.

"I'm Lance by the way," said the man, putting out a hand to him.

"Oh," said Ewan, like this was something unexpected. "I'm Ewan."

He shook the man's hand, letting himself be crushed in his powerful grip, and loving the contact of skin against skin, palm against palm. He wondered what those hands might feel like sliding across the rest of him, and shivered...

"So um... What gave me away?" he gambled, still hoping that he wasn't somehow grossly misinterpreting this whole situation.

Lance raised his eyebrows at him.

"What gave what away?" he asked with a smile.

"Well... That I'm into men," he said, praying that this was actually flirtation, and not some misconstrued friendly gesture that would get him punched in the mouth.

But Lance smiled at his question, and it calmed him down some.

"I guess I just have a nose for that sort of thing," he said. "I'm not too far off, am I?"

Ewan laughed.

"Not far off at all," he admitted. "More like a dead-on bullseye..."

"See," said Lance confidently. "Sometimes a guy just knows things..."

"What else can you tell about me?" Ewan asked, feeling an unusually deep connection with this man. Deeper, in fact, than he usually felt with just about anyone, despite having known him for little more than a matter of minutes.

Lance laughed at this. "Well, I'm not a mind reader," he said. "But... Maybe I picked up on a few things..."

He flared his nostrils again at him, in the same way that had made Ewan feel as unnerved as it had made him horny. His back stiffened as something else did, and he straightened in his seat to try and adjust himself. It was painfully obvious what he was up to, and Lance grinned at it, but mercifully didn't say anything.

"Like what?" Ewan pressed, feeling suddenly like he was under some kind of hot red light, sweltering down on him, yet drawing him toward it, refusing to let him move away.

"Well," said Lance, moving in just a little bit closer. "I can tell from your eyes that you're looking for something. Like a man who isn't totally happy with his life... You think that there's more out there you've been looking for, even though you haven't been able to find it until now..."

"Damn," said Ewan, actually a little bit afraid at how well he'd read him.

"Not too far off base still?"

"Not far at all," said Ewan.

He nodded, smiling. "I've been there," he said. "I know. I know that look. That feeling... I know you're someone who's never totally felt like he belonged, and who's looking for someone to put him in his place. Fill the emptiness that's been hanging over him his entire life..."

"You seem... Awfully sure of yourself," said Ewan, his arousal now unmistakable as Lance drew nearer and nearer to him, his body heat making him sweat, causing his heart to want to break out of his chest.

"And I can tell," he added finally, lifting up a hand without addressing this remark, and placing it gently on the side of his face, "That you're a man who doesn't want to be alone tonight..."

The two men sat looking at one another for a long moment, the heat crackling between them. Ewan felt like he might just about fall backward, and go toppling off of his stool.

Then, when he thought he couldn't stand it anymore, he felt the tips of Lance's fingers pressing against his knee. Felt the palm of his hand sliding warmly up along his thigh, getting him harder and harder as he crept up toward the place between his legs, at last stopping just short before he made it all the way there.

He stared into the man's sharp green eyes, sure this was a mistake, but helpless in his surrender to it.

Then his eyelids closed as he saw the man begin to move toward him. Their lips met.

It was the first man he'd kissed in a very long time...

The flesh of their mouths slid across one another. Lance's stubble prickled against his chin, the side of his face, and he loved it. He wanted to throw himself at him, to wrap himself around him and not let go until the thing building inside him had been unleashed, set off like a bomb, draining away the abundance of tension in his arms and legs and groin.

Lance pushed his tongue into his mouth, and slid it slowly around in his cheeks, the taste of alcohol on one another's breath seeming to make them higher and higher with each passing second.

God it was all moving so fast... Indecently fast, in fact...

Yet he didn't want it to stop. Wanted it to keep on going. Wanted to fling himself forward, headlong, and hurtle into his destruction.

He held against this man for as long as he could stand it, then he pulled away from him, gasping, his eyes wide.

Lance looked over at him, his eyes confident, seeming to say that he'd gotten exactly what he wanted, and that he knew with near certainty that he would end up sealing the deal.

Still, though, he was mindful of Ewan's emotions, and gave him some space. Once his breath had calmed down some he asked, "You alright?"

"Yeah... Yeah," insisted Ewan, nodding. "I'm more than alright, it's just... Fast..."

"Too fast?"

He thought about this. He shook his head, but then said, "I don't really know..."

Lance didn't say anything, but waited for him to elaborate.

Ewan took a while to calm down again, thinking about the question, then tried going into further detail. "It's like... I want it... Part of me wants it... But part of me, is..."

"Afraid?" Lance offered.

He nodded.

"Like I shouldn't want it this fast," he said. "I mean, I don't usually... I don't know what it is about you that- that makes me want it the way I do..."

He knew that the simple act of confessing this was making him vulnerable to this man. He was handing himself over completely, surrendering to whatever perverse intentions Lance might have had, to be controlled and manipulated by him in whatever way his heart happened to desire at the moment.

Yet he couldn't say he really cared...

He wanted it so badly, worse than he'd ever wanted it from anyone before in his life.

Yet he was still far from knowing whether he could trust a man like this with that kind of power over him...

"I understand," said Lance softly. "It might not seem like I do, but... But I do. Better than you could possibly know at this point. I took one look at you, and I knew exactly what kind of man you were. And that I wouldn't be able to stop myself from having you. And that you wouldn't be able to stop yourself from having me, either..."

Ewan laughed at this, and found himself shaking his head, feeling like the world's biggest sucker in that moment.

"God," he said. "I feel like I shouldn't buy a word you're saying to me. I don't know a damn thing about you... But here I am, eating out of the palm of your hand..."

Lance laughed, and a moment later the hand was back on his knee.

"Why don't we get out of here?" he suggested. "And I can show you everything you need to know about me..."

Ewan was speechless.

His mouth opened. It closed.

He couldn't say anything.

He literally couldn't find the words.

He knew, no matter what he said, that he would end up in bed with this man.

He knew that he'd already fallen too far, too fast, and that there was really no hope of tearing himself free of the animal magnetism that now pulled him toward his fate.

Maybe it was the beast inside him, longing to tear free of his cage...

He didn't really know.

All that really remained to be seen as he looked into Lance's eyes, was whether this would end up being the best decision, or the worst mistake of his young life.

Quite possibly, it might end up being both...

Chapter 3

Lance shoved him up against the door of his bedroom like he owned the place- he effectively owned Ewan himself, so it wasn't much of a stretch to consider his home a natural extension of that ownership.

He pinned him up against its surface and kissed him ferociously, licking the insides of his mouth, his hands shimmying along the sides of his body.

Ewan's cock hardened and pressed against his work pants, a moist pool of his desire spread from his tip and bled through the fabric of his underwear. The weight of Lance's body up against it produced a devastating friction as he rubbed it up against his thigh through the man's jeans, and every blessed moment that passed felt like it might well be the one that it all became too much for him.

Lance seemed in total control though, in charge of his each and every movement.

He couldn't genuinely imagine that he was about to let that happen until he'd made that decision himself...

He melted in the man's arms, submitting to him fully and completely. Pressing his hands up beneath the fabric of his t-shirt, feeling the slick carving of his musculature, the heaving stomach, the chiseled abdominals, the delectably cut pectoral muscles. Lance brought his own hands down and slipped them into Ewan's pants. He didn't grab in the center, but slid his palms along his waist and his thighs, coming dangerously close but never quite making it to the center, and this slight holding back became a force that verged on irresistible for him.

He pressed Ewan's head to one side, and sucked hard on the skin of his neck, rolling his tongue along the flesh, sinking his teeth in lightly, making him suffer happily through every glorious moment of it.

Ewan thought he might pass out from the pleasure of it all, and shivered when Lance's hands began to undress him, pulling him out of his shirt, tossing it to the floor, and sliding across his body to admire his own sweet, if slightly lesser musculature. He fondled his chest and his back, sweeping along his spine as they made out, pinching on his nipples, and running kisses from the top of his pecs to the sensitive plain of flesh and muscle just below his belly button.

Ewan nearly thought he was about to go down on him, and was trying to redirect the pressure in his cock to stay hard long enough for him to do so. But before Lance got any further down, he moved back away from him again, standing upright. Ewan thought he might slide down along the door and collapse from the disappointment of it.

"Hey," said Lance, a look of satisfaction on his face at having reduced his prey so thoroughly. "I need to use your bathroom a second before we go any further."

"Oh," said Ewan, nodding. "Yeah, of course. Uh, it's," he started to point to the bathroom door across the room, but then swept a careless hand at it. "Eh, you can find it," he said.

Lance grinned, then gave him another slow kiss on the mouth.

"I won't be long," he said, pulling away from him. "So be ready for me..."

Ewan's cock jumped at this, and his heartbeat raced just a little bit faster.

He watched as Lance slipped off into the bathroom, and stood there for a moment once the door had closed, trying to catch his breath.

He was way too far in to turn back now, he thought to himself, even if he'd had the slightest inclination to do so.

He unstuck his sweat-soaked back from the door and walked over to the bed, pulling back the neatly made silk sheets- he hadn't had the slightest inclination when he'd left it that morning that he'd be returning to it under circumstances even remotely resembling the ones he now faced.

He unbuttoned and unzipped his pants and shucked himself out of them, and stood for a moment in nothing but his underwear. They were a pair of extremely tight, sexy black shorts, through which the vivid impression of his raging boner could be unmistakably made out, his tip peaking out naughtily from the bottom of the right leg. They were the sort of underwear a man buys for a night like the one he was having- that he liked to wear in the seemingly infinitesimal chance that a night like tonight might ever actually happen to him.

He decided not to take them off; that he would much rather have Lance peel the things off of him like a second skin. Or better still, maybe he wouldn't take them off at all, but would mount him with the fabric simply pulled off to one side, giving the whole thing a beautiful sense of desperation and depravity.

He climbed into the covers and buried himself beneath them, then lay waiting anxiously, one hand down his shorts, stroking himself slowly as though the stimulation was necessary to keep him aroused.

He sat there waiting.

And waiting.

The anticipation growing to unbearable heights as the moments passed by.

And then, at last- the bathroom door clicked open.

He sat up, alert, ready to see Lance stepping out naked, showing him the perfect body he'd only had the chance to imagine up until now.

He wasn't at all prepared for what now emerged in his place...

A massive white paw.

Followed by another.

Two long orange legs, nearly as big around as tree trunks.

Attached to an even thicker, golden body, ringed with black stripes. A furry feline face with powerful jaws, and glowing green eyes, and devastating yellow fangs. The body just kept coming and coming, the size of the cat so enormous that Ewan could barely fathom it. At last, an orange, snakelike tail whipped out through the door at the beast's rear end, seeming almost to wave at him, and all Ewan could do was sit there, watching as it paced toward the bed, every bit the predator that he'd imagined it to be.

He couldn't believe it...

He didn't even think it could be possible, and yet here he was, staring at it with his own two eyes.

The beast stepped slowly over to him, its footsteps large, measured, seeming to want to make it known to him that it could lunge for him at any moment, and positively tear him to pieces- if it wanted to.

Ewan followed the creature with his eyes, not even breathing, and watched as its body whipped up into the air, without even needing to build up momentum, and landed down heavily on the foot of his bed. He felt his body drawn toward it as the mattress buckled slightly in the creature's direction, and the two of them simply stared at one another, Ewan unable to contain his astonishment.

At last he spoke, or tried to, stammering, "You're- you're-"

Before he could finish the sentiment, the creature's body began to twist and contort. The hulking cat that had been facing there disappeared. Its frame growing smaller, the fur retreating, the tail dissolving back up into his body.

There was Lance again, naked and perfect, his bare body ringed with tattoos in many of the same places as the tiger, and his glowing green eyes seeming practically unchanged from one state to the other.

"-Like you?" he said, completing Ewan's sentence for him.

Ewan was stunned.

He first gave a single nod, and then shook his head.

"I- how did you know?"

Lance grinned at him.

"Call it instinct, if you want to. There are just some things a shifter knows..."

"I've never told anyone," said Ewan. "I mean, I didn't think I could tell anyone... I didn't think there was anyone who would understand. That there was anyone in the whole world who was like me..."

"You're right about one thing," said Lance. "There aren't a lot of people in this world who would understand. Who would understand what it means to be a tiger shifter, or what it means to be an outsider? To feel like you don't belong where you are, and that you'd rather be anywhere else in the world. But I've felt it before, for so much of my life. And I could see it in your eyes, back at the bar. I could smell it on you... And I knew, almost immediately- here's someone who understands... Here's someone who's alone, who I can be together with. Even if it's just for one night, or whatever this might turn into. But I knew... I knew exactly what I wanted, the moment I saw you. And I knew it was exactly what you wanted, too..."

Ewan didn't say anything.

He was silent, for a long, long time.

It didn't seem to be the reaction Lance was hoping for.

He edged back a little bit on the bed, trying to give him some space.

"I hope this isn't too much for you," he said, once the silence had dragged on too long.

Ewan waited, and waited, staring off into the distance. Then he looked up at him, shaking a little bit.

"Take me," he said simply.

Lance raised an eyebrow at him.

"Sorry?" he asked.

"Take me," he repeated.

"You're right," he said simply, shaking his head. "What more is there to say about it? You're right. About everything... And now I don't think I can go on a minute longer unless you make me yours."

Lance grinned, and took a deep breath.

Then he climbed up onto him, and slipped beneath the covers beside him.

They began to kiss.

To touch.

To caress one another.

Lance's mouth tasted even sweeter against him than it had before. The way it rolled around inside his mouth. The way it pushed back inside his throat.

His body heaved gently on top of him as they kissed, his powerful muscles washing over him, the friction of their bodies incredible, making Ewan feel totally helpless beneath the bulk of his perfect weight. His long, rigid cock slid across the course of Ewan's heaving stomach, his warm balls rolling along his skin. His jizz seeped out along his abs, coating him with the sweet, glistening fluid, and Ewan could feel the pressure growing inside his own loins, begging to be released.

Perceiving his need, Lance plunged a firm hand down into his underwear, wrapping his fingers tight around his burning cock, and holding it tight like a weapon. A spasm of pleasure burned through Ewan's body, and he stiffened beneath Lance's weight, in more ways than one.

He smiled malevolently down at him.

"I bet you've never known what it's like to be loved by an alpha male before, have you?" he asked.

"No," Ewan gasped, his voice almost pleading. "Never..."

Slowly Lance began to pump him in his hand, pushing the warm loose flesh around the hard, throbbing core, squeezing his balls as he pushed the skin all the way down. The pressure was delectable, the concentrated grasp of that tight hand around his burning manhood turning the rest of his body to putty in his grip. He let out a deep moan, and Lanced took this as a sign to keep going, pushing harder, faster, deeper, getting him nice and long and stiff in his grip.

"Then get ready," he said, "Because I've been looking for a man like you for a long time. And I have absolutely no intention of taking things easy on you..."

"Do your worst," Ewan gasped, not sure, even as he said it, whether this was a gamble he was genuinely prepared to make.

Ready or not, he was about to find out...

Lance's strokes grew longer, harder, more intense. He slammed his clenched fist down against Ewan's pelvis, stretching the flesh vigorously, building him up like an active volcano. Ewan kept having to jerk his body up from the bed to regulate the sensations, praying that each vicious spasm of pleasure wouldn't be the one to set him over the edge. It didn't help when, perceiving his struggle, Lance brought his lips down to the front of Ewan's body, kissing his chest and his stomach as he masturbated him. Each warm dissolution of that glorious mouth against his flesh was like twisting the dagger into his rapidly beating heart, making him want it more and more. His breathing grew deeper and deeper, his nostrils flaring, his chest heaving as he struggled to contain himself.

He noticed, as it wore on, that Lance's lips were creeping further and further south along his body, growing nearer and nearer toward a particular target- the very same one presently being manipulated by his tightly cupped hand.

He took in a deep breath of air, trying to brace himself, but aware, even as he did so, that there was really no use in even attempting it.

He felt the warm glide of Lance's tongue as it pressed between his testicles, rolling across his hot, tight sack as though it was the most delectable thing he'd ever tasted. Ewan moaned, tilting his head back as Lance sucked each nut into his mouth. Then he rolled his tongue slowly up, up, up along the expanse of his penis, lapping up every inch of him as he went. He took his hand and spread the saliva up and down along him several times, then lowered his head and slid the tip between his lips.

His mouth melted around him, hot and wet and a perfectly tight seal. Ewan's ass tightened up hard, and something primitive and animalistic stirred deep inside him, as though awakened for the very first time in his life. He closed his eyes and savored the feeling of it, the syrupy perfection of Lance's face as it melted down along him, swallowing every glorious inch of that immaculate shaft.

He touched down against his pelvis, and smothered his face in Ewan's loins, rolling his tongue around him and making him squirm beneath the force of his efforts.

"Oh, God," Ewan gasped, his teeth actually beginning to chatter as the sensations penetrated him.

Lance pulled up slightly on him, making him jerk up from the bed, but then pushed back down into his lap before going any further. He pulled up again, reproducing the effect, but then buried his face in his lap once more. He repeated it a few times, driving Ewan crazy, then at last he brought his face all the way up along the length of him, pulling back all the way to his engorged purple tip.

"Oh, God," Ewan choked, the pressurized vacuum around his head almost more than he could stand.

Lance held and held, then snapped his lips away, grinning up at him.

"You like that, don't you?" he said, then he took him back in his hand again to straighten him out for consumption, and pressed his face forward again, engulfing him once more.

He sucked hard, and deep, and fast.

His entire weight heaved through the air, his head bobbing steadily in Ewan's lap, pushing him to his utmost limits. Small, desperate moans of pleasure kept escaping through his lips in spite of himself, and Lance seemed to love it whenever this took place, upping his pace, his speed, his depth, making it even harder for him to withstand it.

How could something so perfect, so exactly what he needed in that moment, have been delivered to him so suddenly, almost without warning, Ewan wondered? Was it simply fate?

For as little as he knew about this man, the connection he'd felt when their eyes met across the room had been deep and instantaneous, and the feeling he now experienced, with his lips wrapped so tightly around him, was an intimacy of a sort he might never have imagined possible in the past.

Lance's face just kept coming and coming, his throat seemingly endless as he continued going down on him, the inside of his mouth grazing him so beautifully that his destruction became little more than an inevitability.

And then it came.

As though perfectly able to calculate the timing, Lance shoved his middle finger up the tight hole between Ewan's open legs, while simultaneously yanking back on the flesh and holding him with the utmost pressure.

The pleasure exploded in Ewan's body. It started in his backside then burned up from the base of his cock to its tip, erupting in a fountain of his hot, pearly white sperm. It gushed in abundance into Lance's open mouth, filling up his cheeks, spilling back down over Ewan's springing penis as it continued to erupt in his mouth.

"Yes... Yes... Yes..." Ewan moaned, his buttocks clenched, his fingers curling into the bedspread, and the entire room seemed to spin around him. In those sweet, perfect moments, everything he was became concentrated in that perfect, molten flow into his partner's mouth, as though nothing else, in the whole wide world, could possibly matter.

At last, he felt himself becoming gradually drained, and he rested his head back down on the sweat-soaked pillow, his heart hammering, his body trembling.

Lance brought his face back down into his lap, then pulled his head slowly up along him, rolling his tongue around the shaft as though to collect every last drop of him he might have missed.

He pulled his lips away, letting some of Ewan's cum drip from his mouth onto his stubbled chin. Ewan thought it was the hottest thing he'd ever seen as he lay there, spent and panting. It was nothing, though, compared to when Lance put his hands on him, and flipped him over onto his stomach on the bed. He pressed open his ass, then pressed his face between his open buttocks and poured his fluid back into him, pushing the hot semen into his tight anus with his wet, lapping tongue.

Ewan started, his breath growing short and quick as Lance ate his ass, lubricating him with his own ejaculate. He pushed it in and twisted it around, and it took an immense effort for Ewan to keep from crying out, as though he had any real reason for restraining himself.

His tongue felt so incredible, pushing around inside him, opening him up, sliding its way in and dipping back out...

He'd gone semi-flaccid from that first insane orgasm, but he could already feel himself getting hard again, aroused as he was by the sweetness of Lance's efforts.

Lance continued to eat him out, nodding his head, seeming to savor every inch of him, until every last ounce of his warm substance had been pressed back into his body. Once he was finished, he lifted Ewan up onto his hands on knees on the bed, then climbed up onto his back, wrapping his legs around him. He slid his cock up and down between the open cheeks of his ass, making him quake beneath his weight. He reached beneath him and took his growing cock in his hand, fondling him gently, as up above he ran gentle kisses along the course of his neck.

"Now that I've got you nice and warmed up," he whispered into his ear. "Do you think you're finally ready to be taken like the animal you are?"

"Yes," pleaded desperately, nearly gasping out the word. "More ready than I've ever been for anything in my entire life..."

Lance smiled at this.

He held the skin of Ewan's erection all the way back, and angled himself into position.

Ewan felt the hot tip of his cock lining up against his dripping hole, its head just barely peeking in through the tight opening of his ass.

He waited, building up the anticipation.

Then he pushed himself in.

Ewan gasped.

His body lunged forward, and then relaxed back, letting him inside.

The tunnel of his ass was filled by the oncoming train of Lance's incredible masculinity, pumping up into him, pumping him up to his full and utter capacity. It stretched out the walls of his ass, and set him alight with sensations, his swollen tip smashing down against his prostate, making his cock leap violently in Lance's hand.

Once he was in he let out a deep sigh, his eyes wide, his limbs trembling, his head swimming from the sensations. Lance breathed heavily down onto his neck, savoring the heat of his ass. Then he ran a series of soft, gentle kisses along his shoulders, a gesture far more intimate than their acquaintance seemed to warrant.

And yet, Ewan thought, he really kind of liked it...

Lance held in him until they'd both grown accustomed to one another. Then, very slowly, he drew himself back out again, extricating himself nearly all the way to his tip. He hovered there, letting the moment build. Then he slammed himself forward, striking down much harder before against the tender magic of Ewan's prostate.

He cried out, and again his dick sprang up in Lance's fingers.

Lance cupped his hand back against him, pulling his body toward himself, and began to fuck him, holding him totally captive beneath his pounding weight. Thrusting, heaving, burying every inch of himself up the ass of his omega, he tore into Ewan for all that he was worth, savoring the pressure of their colliding bodies, the slamming of muscle into muscle, the mutual burning of their loins as they hammered into one another, chiseling away like there was no tomorrow.

Ewan's ass bounced as Lance's powerful body smacked repeatedly into it, the sound roaring like thunderclaps in his ears. He dug his fingers into the sheets in a meager attempt to keep himself in place, but found that he could barely hold on, overwhelmed as he was by every thrust, every movement, every collision of flesh into flesh, man into man- not to mention, by the continued, vigorous jacking of Lance's clenched fist around his cock, adding the pressure of frontal stimulation to his sweet, relentless ass-ramming.

It was all very quickly becoming too much for him...

The bed shook beneath their heaving weight. The sounds of percussively slapping flesh boomed through the air. The scent of sheer animal lust wafted into both men's nostrils, adding unspeakable pleasure to the already intense mix of their love, until finally it came to the point that neither of them could stand it any longer.

With a last, mighty force, Lance crushed himself up inside of Ewan's body, forcing in every inch of himself, and Ewan cried out even louder than before. He felt the hot, vigorous pelting of his alpha's sperm against the inside of his ass, Lance growling at first, then roaring like the beast that he was, the alpha male, taking total and complete control of his prey. It poured into him in thick, hot abundance, coating the inside of his ass, spilling out of him in its abundance onto his nuts, and dripping down onto the bed beneath their shifting, trembling weight.

His cock leapt again with the thrill of orgasm, an even thicker, more intense stream of his essence shooting out as Lance continued to inseminate him, their bodies locked in sweet, carnal union as the pleasure flowed back and forth between them as though in a circuit, shining through every muscle, every nerve ending, shaking both men to their very deepest cores.

At last, when everything they had to offer had been drained from them, the two of them, alpha and omega, collapsed down onto the surface of the bed, panting and exhausted, but their bodies seeming to glow with pleasure as they basked in the afterglow of their lovemaking.

Ewan still didn't know entirely where he stood with the man who'd just taken him as he'd done, and so he was mildly surprised when he felt Lance's arm lacing around his midriff, pulling him back into himself in a way that was almost romantic. The alpha male spooned his omega from behind, and whispered gently into his ear.

"Like I said back at the bar," he said, "It looked like you needed that."

Ewan grinned at him, and peered into those emerald green eyes.

"And like I said," he teased, "I'm pretty sure that you're a mind-reader..."

And with that, the two men curled up into one another's arms, kissing and caressing one another deep into the night.

Chapter 4

Ewan had been a bit surprised to find Lance still lying beside him the next morning. He'd practically expected him to go bolting off the moment he'd fallen asleep, though he'd been hoping to be proven wrong on that front.

Once he was up, they both lay in bed talking and lazing in the golden morning sunlight, feeling a bit dreamy, as though lost in a trance, and neither of them in any great hurry to find their way out of it.

Lance told him about his past. About being an alpha male to a hidden Streak of tiger shifters, and always feeling as though the world was too small for him. Believing that there almost certainly had to be something more for him out there, if only there was some way for him to figure out what it was.

Ewan said he understood in a way, and that he'd gone through a kind of similar experience in his own life, if perhaps in a slightly different direction.

"I'm not sure how old I was when I knew," he said, looking off into the distance. "I mean, even when I was a kid, I could tell that I was different from other kids. Like there was something I had to hide, but I don't know... I guess part of it was not knowing who my parents were- I was adopted when I was a baby. So it didn't really feel like I belonged anywhere."

"You belong right here," said Lance, pulling him back into his chest, and wrapping his legs around him from behind. Ewan smiled, and was quite long enough for Lance to crane over his shoulder and kiss him, slowly, passionately on the lips.

Was this love, he wondered?

Better not to think about that sort of thing this early on...

It was clear, though, no matter what happened from this point onward, that the two of them shared a special connection. Something that went far deeper than just sex, as amazing as the physical sensations of the previous night had truly been.

Ewan thought for a while longer as Lance's fingers slid across his chest. Then he turned back around and asked, still not wholly able to grasp the concept, "So there are really more like us out there? A world full of tiger shifters, that I never even knew about until now?"

Lance nodded. He didn't seem too eager to discuss the subject, but Ewan couldn't help but ask questions.

"I've always dreamed there could be somewhere like that out there," he continued. "I mean, the first time I transformed as a kid, it kind of just scared the hell out of me. I mean, it would any kid who didn't know what was happening to them... I can't even begin to imagine how much easier it would all have been for me. Not feeling all the time like I was some weird outsider. Like there were actually people out there who were different like I was... How many people, would you say-?"

Before he could finish this sentence, Lance was already leaning into him again, kissing the back of his neck. His lips were hot and wet, and sent shivers running along Ewan's spine.

"Let's not talk about that right now, okay? I just want to focus on what's right here, right now, between the two of us."

Ewan closed his mouth, a little bit disappointed, his curiosity too piqued to willingly drop the subject that easily.

Then, however, he felt the grip of Lance's fingers wrapping around the shaft of his cock, pressing the warm skin between his fingers, and pumping it slowly back and forth, all while gently squeezing his scrotum below.

A shudder of breath escaped from his lungs, and he knew there was no real point in continuing this conversation at the moment.

Lance was right, and he was more than happy to trade rumination about the past for his present dissolving like putty in his hand...

———

Because of who he was, and the life he'd lived up until now, Ewan had always been wary whenever it came to matters of the heart. "Love" felt like a concept that only existed in songs and in movies, and in real life it seemed like little more than a hazard, a threat to his very continued existence.

But he fell to it fast once Lance entered into his life, surrendering to his passions as though resisting for so long had been nothing more than a pretense. He was Lance's, and Lance's was his, and the world had never looked so bright...

For the first time in- well, in forever- Ewan had been taking time off of his work, just so he could destress and spend some time with the incredible new man who'd entered so unexpectedly into his life. Lance had been working as a bouncer at a club ever since he'd made his flight from the Streak, and working only nights, his daytime schedule was always especially flexible.

For those first few glorious weeks, the two men spent as much time in one another's company, doing anything and everything they could think of together, and sometimes being content to simply do absolutely nothing at all.

They went on walks together, strolling together beneath the afternoon sunlight without a care in the world. Or else on runs, sprinting through the park in their human forms, mutually trying to outdo one another and both prove themselves the stronger, faster man. Almost invariably it was Lance who won these competitions, alpha male that he was, but once in a while Ewan managed to come in first (though he suspected happily that when this was the case, it was because Lance himself had intentionally let him when.)

They went out to dinner together and sat talking and laughing for hours, getting drunk and feasting on something raw and meaty, usually steak- which made Ewan feel even more like the bloodthirsty beast he was becoming.

They went out to movies together, too- the very concept of a motion picture seemed fascinating to Lance, having been deprived of such luxuries his entire life as a forest dwelling tiger shifter. He seemed to request that they go out to the cinema as often as possible, and Ewan couldn't say that he minded all that much. After all, it gave him the perfect excuse to spend a solid two hours with his head on Lance's chest, listening to the sound of his beating heart, as the movie flashed absently onscreen in front of them...

Then, on top of these and a million and a half other things, there was the six.

The long, steamy, delectable sex.

Hours on end spent writhing passionately beneath the sheets. Twisting. Scratching. Tearing at one another. Ewan, reclaiming his animal nature as he surrendered his body to Lance, fully and completely. Lance, reclaiming his status as an alpha, even among the human world, by dominating his partner so thoroughly and completely, causing every inch of him to tremble with longing and exhaustion, drenching every space of flesh on his body with sweat and saliva and his other potent fluid...

As innocent as their love might have seemed on a day to day basis, there was nothing at all innocent about what they did to one another in bed. The cries of ecstasy. The tearing, the biting, the clawing of flesh. The spasms of pleasure, the hot waves of orgasm, the exchange of essence between one man and the other, hot, wet, and abundant, their capacity for such wild, drawn out lust seemingly without end.

Every day they woke up together in one another's arms, ready to face the day together.

Every night they wound up slamming the bed against the wall as they fucked one another's lights out, as addicted to one another's bodies as they were their minds, and only too happy to continue the cycle of awakening in their mutual embrace whenever the next morning came.

It was a beautiful cycle to be enshrined in, and one that they often believed they might never want to be free of.

Not everything was all sunshine and roses, though...

As close as they were to one another on so many levels, and as hard and as quickly as they'd fallen for each other, it was still hard to entirely get around certain issues regarding the differences in their background.

Specifically, the issue of Lance's homeland, and his former Streak, which Ewan seemed always to want to discuss, and which Lance seemed sick and tired of ever hearing about it again.

He had, after all, come to the human world to be free of all that. He wanted to put it all behind him, pretend that the past never happened, in order to move forward and preserve his own sanity. It bothered him to no end how insistent Ewan was that he discuss the details of his discarded shell of a life, anytime there was any kind of lull in the conversation.

How many of you were there?

You mean shifter society is all male, and no females?

Are there other groups of us in the world, or is it just the one that you know of?

What sort of duties did you have as a high alpha?

On and on these interrogations went. In all likelihood, the questions were asked in total innocence, without any implications made about Lance or his running away from home. To him, though, the undertone was always the same, perhaps more from his own sense of guilt, than from anything done wrong on Ewan's part.

How could you have left them that way?

How could a leader turn his back on his people, just so he could pursue his own selfish interests?

You turned your back on them for no good reason, and now you're pretending like they don't even exist?

How could I ever love a man like you?

How could I ever trust you not to do the same thing to me?

Invariably, these rounds of questioning led to arguments between the two men- sometimes quite explosive in nature.

There would be yelling, pounding of fists against the walls on both sides, and often it grew so bad that the men couldn't even remember what they'd begun fighting about in the first place.

The best fights often ended up in the throes of angry, delirious sex, with Lance taking Ewan vigorously up the ass, often far harder than he did normally. He sometimes suspected that Ewan even provoked him on purpose in this way, just to gain access to the intense pleasure of their make-up fucking whenever it inevitably rolled around in the end.

Even so, there was really no doubting the fact that his underlying curiosity was sincere...

All in all, though, even with some of the turbulence that plagued them, Lance and Ewan's burgeoning relationship was generally a happy one, the highs of their shared bliss generally overshadowing the moments of turbulence that sometimes came between them.

For the longest time, it didn't seem possible to Ewan that the happiness they shared could ever really end.

And then he got pregnant...

Unsurprisingly, he didn't believe it at first.

He didn't accept that that could possibly be what it was- he couldn't accept it, in fact. He'd been feeling sick in the mornings, and could feel the physical changes beginning inside him, but it didn't seem like it could possibly be real.

It wasn't until he saw his reflection in the mirror one morning, his belly gradually beginning to swell up like a balloon, that it dawned on him that his condition was very much a real one, and that one way or another he was going to have to deal with the issue...

Lance had told him, after all, hadn't he?

That shifter society was all male?

How else could they have reproduced, if not for the aid of male pregnancy?

Why he never suspected that such a thing could happen to him was difficult to fathom exactly, he wasn't sure. Maybe the concept was just entirely too alien to him for it to ever seem that real, and as a result he'd never taken the proper precautions to prevent it from happening.

And now, because of that very arrogance, he found himself standing face to face with the consequences, unsure of exactly where to turn.

One thing he did know, regardless of whether or not he decided to keep the baby, was that the human world that had been rejecting him for the past two decades was no place at all to raise a child like the one growing inside him...

He knew that, if he was going to carry this baby to term, it would have to be somewhere far away. Somewhere the child might ever have a chance to felt he truly belonged, where he wouldn't feel the way Ewan had done all that time- like an outsider, a pariah. A reject.

He knew that there was only one option. That if his developing son was ever going to have anything resembling a real life in this world, there was only one place they could go.

And he knew, even before speaking a single word to the effect, exactly what Lance's reaction would be to such a proposition...

———

They were lying in bed one night in a damp tangle of sheets. They'd just finished making love, and Ewan's body still tingled with the ecstasy of sensation, his loins still burning as he tried to ease his way down from the heights of euphoria. Throughout it all, however, it had been as though he wasn't entirely there. Like he was distant, detached, the sweetness of a Lance-induced orgasm the only thing that even came close to pulling him back down to earth.

Now he lay with his head on Lance's chest, tracing out the lines of his black-striped tattoos with his fingertips. Lance was looking down at him, running his fingers slowly through his blonde hair, and sniffing it gently, loving the scent.

"What's wrong?" he asked finally, and Ewan looked up at him.

"What?" he asked, pretending for some reason that nothing was up.

"You seem distracted... I mean, even through all that..." He smirked a little bit as he said this, as though wondering how anyone could possibly remain distracted by the intensity of such vigorous lovemaking as the sort they'd just completed.

Ewan shrugged. "Oh."

"Is something on your mind?" Lance pressed.

"I don't know," he said, looking away. For some reason, he didn't quite feel like revealing the pregnancy to him just yet. He wanted to keep it close to him, as though by doing so the power of decision making could remain in his hands. First, he thought, he should gauge how he would react to his potential plan for the future. See what he thought of it, and whether the life he needed to provide for his child could even be a possibility.

"You can tell me," said Lance. "Whatever it is..."

He sighed.

"Well... It's just... Do you ever think about- going back?"

He still wasn't looking back at him, but he almost immediately felt the rise and fall of his chest beneath him cease. Like he'd tensed up at the query, annoyed by the very fact of him having asked.

"No," he said tensely. "I don't. And I think you know that by now..."

At this, Ewan turned back to look at him, pulling up off of his chest. His face was stern. His eyes cold.

"Oh," said Ewan. "Because... Well... Sometimes... Maybe I do..." He said it with more bitterness than he'd originally intended. He'd meant to bring it up gently, ease him into it. But there was something about Lance's harshness that made him want to rise to meet it, sabotaging his efforts before they'd even truly begun.

"I think, by now," said Lance, sitting up in the bed, and their warm, wet bodies separated, for what they didn't know would be the last time in a very last time, "That I've made myself very clear in that regard..."

Ewan narrowed his eyes at him. The angrier he got, the angrier it made him. Why the hell did he get so unreasonable about this subject? Why did he feel the need to shoot down his plan before it even made it past his lips?

"Yes," said Ewan, "You've made yourself very, very clear... So clear, in fact, that I've never had the chance to tell you how I feel about the subject. How I might want, for the first time in my life, to feel like I lived somewhere that I belonged. Among my own kind."

Lance's expression hardened still further, his jaws clenched.

"You don't belong there," he said, getting defensive. Ewan thought he could see a tinge of fear in his eyes, coloring his true reasons for being this way. He wanted to keep Ewan under his thumb. He didn't want to lose him.

But this possessiveness, sometimes an unbearable attraction, was suddenly seeming like petty arrogance in his eyes, and not something he was about to stand for.

"No," said Ewan, shaking his head. "You don't belong there. And you're too afraid of owning up to your own dumb mistakes to let me find out for myself..."

"I would watch your fucking tone if I were you..." said Lance, his eyes narrowed.

And it was all downhill from there...

Soon, the two men were shouting at each other, tapping into their deepest animosities in a mutual effort to tear one another down to their foundations.

It wasn't just Ewan's wanderlust.

It was every fight they'd ever had up until now, rolled into one.

It was every difference of opinion. Every night Ewan wanted to stay in and nest when Lance wanted to go out drinking together. Every mess Lance refused to clean up. Every single goddamn time Ewan brought up the subject of the Streak, even though he could see clearly how much it bothered Lance to remember.

"I don't think you ever loved me at all!" Lance had thundered, towering over him. "You just loved the fucking Streak, and saw me as a way to escape your miserable, pathetic life and get to them!"

Naturally, Lance had argued back against this point, but deep down he couldn't help but wonder if maybe there was some grain of truth to his words...

Never once, throughout the course of the shouting match that ensued, did Ewan bring up the subject of his pregnancy, as close as it came to the tip of his tongue on numerous occasions. Maybe he was just too angry, but telling Lance felt like conceding something to him, giving over a part of himself that he didn't come close to deserving.

"Fine!" he shouted at last, storming out of bed toward the door, and not even bothering to put his clothes on. He wouldn't need them where he was going... "If that's the way you want it, then that's the way you can have it! Spend your entire life alone if you want to, cut off from the only place in this world where you belong! Isolate yourself until you're old and miserable, and then spend your dying days wondering where the hell you went wrong! But don't expect to have me there by your side, because I'm done with that shit! I've been doing it for twenty years, and I'm fucking done with it!"

He marched toward the door, but was stopped by the sudden, indelicate grip of a hand around his grip.

"Don't you walk out that fucking door!" Lance commanded him, and in a normal fight this might be the point where they fell into one another's arms, and started furiously, passionately fucking.

But this wasn't a normal fight, and the look in Lance's eyes was anything but a normal one...

He looked crazed, like a man who would do anything to keep him from leaving. He looked, in fact, like he might transform at any second and try to physically prevent Ewan's departure.

It was, for Ewan, the point of no return...

"Get your goddamn hands off me..." he seethed, his voice as sharp and as cold as the steely blade of a knife.

He jerked his arm viciously back, the veins still throbbing from the pain of Lance's fingertips. Then, paying him a last cold look, he spun around on his heels, and leapt through the air. His body twisted and writhed, and by the time he hit the ground he'd entered into his tiger form, landing on all fours, and bounding toward the door.

Lance panicked.

He jumped up off of the bed, skidding on the sheets as he transformed as well, then he thundered forward in Ewan's wake, scrambling to catch him.

He didn't know what his plan was.

Tackle him? Hold him captive there by nothing but his own brute strength?

He drew in close, so close that he could hear the ripple of Ewan's fur against his face, but then tripped over his own two front paws before he had the chance to bridge the gap between them. He skidded across the living room rug. He uprighted himself just in time to see Ewan speeding out through the front door, racing down the hallway without once looking back.

Dear God, he thought- what the hell had he done?

Ashamed of himself- his hotheadedness and his aggression, and the hateful way he'd spoken to the man he loved- he rose back up onto his haunches, and shifted again into his human form. He ran for the door, and stood naked at the threshold, calling after the huge striped cat now bounding toward the stairs of the apartment complex.

"Ewan! Ewan wait, come back! I'm so sorry!"

But it was entirely too late for him to change what had already been set in motion...

Ewan didn't even look back.

He would never look back again, he decided in that moment.

He ran for the exit as though his very life depended on it.

Ran as though he might never stop running again. Or at least, not until he'd put as much distance as possible between himself and the man in his apartment.

As much distance as possible between himself and the life he was leaving behind...

He didn't think about where he was going as he ran, though he had a fairly definite idea as to where that might be.

He just kept running. And running. And running.

He ran until his legs felt like they might buckle out from under him, and even then he just kept running, not really giving a damn in that moment whether the effort of doing so killed him.

He ran by instinct, only half paying any sort of attention to where he was going, closing his eyes and surrendering himself fully to the void.

Only when he opened his eyes again did he begin to slow down.

His run slowed to a trot, then to a walk, and then gradually his feet came to a rest against the crunch of leaves beneath him.

His legs shook, the muscles feeling as though they'd been set alight, with a fire that might never be extinguished.

He looked about at his surroundings, the visuals alien and unfamiliar, but the scent one that he'd known his entire life.

He'd never been here before, yet he was sure he knew exactly where he was.

And then he heard the sound of footsteps...

He turned, and watched the materialization of an oversized feline form from out of the shadows, the green eyes glowing, a long tail whipping softly behind it in the darkness.

On either side of it, two more cats crept toward him, and Ewan turned again to see that a whole circle of tigers had emerged, creeping toward him in the moonlight, surrounding him on all sides.

His throat tightened, and he felt his hair bristling. He felt cautious, on edge- but not entirely afraid.

He waited, as dozens of the creatures appeared as though from thin air, calling themselves up into existence from nothing. Then, at last, when there was no place for him to run if he wanted to, a final cat made its way forward through the others. It was the largest of them all, comparable in size only to Lance, whose shifter form was considerably larger than Ewan's own.

The high alpha, he thought...

The cat circled slowly around him like the beast of prey he was, performing an inventory on all sides. Ewan trembled, but tried to remain steady. The more panic he showed, the weaker he would look.

He needed to stay calm, and not allow his anxiety to shine through...

The tiger made several trips around him, feeling more and more like a vulture with every lap he made. Then, at last, he stopped, standing in front of him, locking him in those ghostly yellow eyes of his.

He rose up onto his haunches.

The body shrank, though only by degrees, as it became transfigured into the sculpted physique of a naked human man, towering up over him, his bright eyes no less piercing in the thorough darkness that enveloped them.

He watched. And waited.

Then he smiled, and Ewan felt something giving way inside his chest.

"Welcome home, child," said the man, in a firm, reassuring voice.

It was the first time in his life that Ewan had ever truly understood what "home" truly meant...

Chapter 5

Lance stood at the forest's edge, his heart pumping angrily in his throat.

A soft breeze blew against his back, as though encouraging to take the first crucial step. But he nevertheless remained planted firmly to the spot, his force of will refusing to surrender to what he knew needed to be done.

A year had passed.

More than a year, really.

Time had ceased to have much meaning since the night Ewan had left. The days all sort of blended together, and lost any sense of purpose they might once have had.

Every night he lay awake, playing over the words they'd exchanged in that last, wretched fight they'd had. All the horrible things he'd said, playing back in a loop, as though on some tape recorder in his head that couldn't be shut off.

He'd tried so hard, for so long, to drown it all out.

He'd turned to drink. To the beds of other men. He'd even given drugs a shot for a while, but they only made him more miserable.

He kept trying to tell himself that it had been nothing but a fling. That he would simply move on from it as he'd moved on from so many other meaningless flings in his life.

But there was no moving on from Ewan.

No convincing himself that what they'd shared was simply some dumb fling...

He sighed, and shook his head.

He knew what he needed to do. He'd known ever since the night he'd left. Knew exactly where he could find the man he loved, exactly what he needed to say to him.

Yet he'd never found it within himself to do so...

He'd never had the strength, the fortitude he needed to confront his past. To return to the forest that had confined him for so long, that he'd abandoned in his desperation.

Even though that same forest had taken possession of the one thing in the world he couldn't possibly live without, and the only way he could possibly reclaim him was to enter it, even if it killed him.

He'd been far too weak, for far too long.

But now he simply couldn't stand it anymore...

He still felt too weak. Like there was a very real chance that the effort might destroy him.

But he knew he would be left even weaker by Ewan's continued absence. Even more incapable of moving on with his life.

He needed to have him back again. Needed to reclaim- no, not reclaim- to redeem himself in the eyes of the man he loved.

He needed to confront the past, after all this time, if he wanted to have any hope in hell of a future with Ewan.

Or any kind of a future at all...

He took a deep breath.

He closed his eyes, and counted off the moments, with no perceivable endpoint in mind.

Then he transformed, and leapt into the darkness.

The time for doubt, for any kind of weakness, was entirely long gone.

It was time for him to do what he should have done more than a year ago...

———

Ewan sat in the room of his little hut, a small, writhing tangle of life pressed against his chest. Colin, his pride and joy. The light of his life, following the period of such thorough darkness that had consumed him. The baby's legs kicked and spasmed, but very slowly, the energy seemed to drain away from him. Sleep took over, and aside from a few soft breaths and hiccups, the movement at last ceased.

Ewan smiled, and placed the little wonder softly down in his crib, planting a gentle kiss in the center of his forehead.

Colin twitched in his sleep, and Ewan thought he could feel his heart breaking just a little bit as he watched him there, so fragile, so innocent.

He stepped back from the crib, and sighed.

For the millionth time over, he tried to tell himself that he'd made the right decision. That leaving Lance behind, and along with him the entire human world, had been the best thing for the both of them.

But God, how he wished the child's father could be in his life.

For that matter, how badly he wished that Lance could still be in his own life, to fill the parallel voids of fear and uncertainty that had crept over him in the year since they'd become separated.

In so many ways, he knew, things were better here for Colin than they would have been in the human world. It was a bit primitive, to be sure, without the technological advances and creature comforts of the world he left behind. But more importantly, here he could be among his own kind. He didn't ever have to worry about being persecuted for his differences, or have his life put at risk for the fact of his being a tiger-shifter.

He could live wild and free, the same way Ewan had always longed to live, and that he was finally able to do for the very first time in his life.

Yes, he told himself... He'd made the right decision, even if the loneliness of it sometimes got to him, and he worried about his son growing up without an alpha figure to look up to in his life.

But then again, it wasn't as though Ewan was lacking for attention from the other strong males of the Streak...

Even despite his pregnancy, many of the other tiger shifters had shown visible attraction to him ever since his arrival. Ulric in particular, the Streak's high alpha ,had seemed especially interested in getting to know him. He didn't know exactly how he felt about this, to be honest- there were times when he seemed like a bit of an asshole to those around him, though he supposed maybe that was sometimes an unfortunate necessity when you held any kind of leadership position. He'd always been nice to Ewan though, giving him a place to live and making sure his needs were met, as well as the needs of his child. There was also just something about him- maybe a kind of alpha strength that reminded him of Lance- that admittedly got Ewan more than just a little bit hot and bothered when he wasn't careful.

It was all still too soon for him, though...

He'd only delivered Colin a few short months ago, and he was really still adjusting to everything- his new life among shifter society, as well as the absence of the man he once loved- to even think about dipping his toes in the water when it came to dating.

It was strange, he thought- he'd been apart from Lance for far longer than the two of them had ever been together. That really depressed him, and he wished he could either move on or somehow reconcile the whole situation...

And then suddenly- as though in acknowledgement of the fact that he'd just been ruminating about the whole mess he was in (though this was far from unusual for him these days)- a familiar, long lost scent drifted into his nostrils.

He paused.

He straightened up, and furrowed his brow.

"No... It couldn't be," he said.

It must just be his mind playing tricks on him, his desperation growing far too powerful for him to resist any longer...

And yet, nevertheless, here he now found himself, stepping out of his hut, craning his neck around as he tried to sniff out the source.

It was coming from the woods beyond the clearing, still a ways off, but coming nearer...

Damn it, he thought, excited but afraid. It was, after all, what he'd been waiting for for over a year now. Yet he knew he was in no way prepared to handle it.

He thought for a moment, then turned back to see three men standing a bit away around a roaring fire, talking and laughing, and probably a little bit drunk.

He tapped one of the men on the shoulder, a beta male he'd become acquaintances with, and who he suspected might have a little bit of a thing for him.

"Hey, Randall... Do you think you could do me a favor and keep an eye on Colin, just for a few minutes? I need to go out and tend to something?"

"Yeah, sure, I'd be happy to," he said, and Ewan was happy to perceive that he seemed the least drunk of the three companions.

Once the man was in place in Ewan's hut, he took off in the direction of the scent, wanting for some reason to head him off before he made it all the way into the village. Honestly, he wasn't sure he was ready for him to know about Colin just yet, and given his contempt for the life he'd left behind, he didn't really think he would mind all that much.

He ran through the darkness, his heart racing, a million thoughts, a million things he felt he needed to say swirling around inside his mind.

It was only when the two tigers emerged into a clearing, standing there, facing one another, that he knew that not a word he'd had in mind would do him the least iota of good.

All he could do was stand there in his astonishment, as he gazed panting at the man who was his complement. The man who'd completed him as no one else had ever been able to, and then left him with a hole in his life that could never be filled.

A long silence ensued between the two of them. Nothing stirred. There wasn't a sound to be heard beyond the gentle chirping of insects in the still, empty night.

Then, Lance moved.

He rose up.

Transformed.

Displayed the beautiful body that Ewan had come to miss so desperately, firm and striped and leading him almost helplessly into temptation.

He maintained his resolve, though. Decided it was in his best interest not to falter, or to give in to him too quickly.

He transformed as well, and didn't say anything.

It was Lance who spoke first.

"I've been a fool," he said, his voice thick with remorse.

"Yes," said Ewan cruelly. "I'm glad to see you've come around to the fact."

"Every day," he said, shaking his head. "Every day, and every night. You're all I've been able to think about. You, and everything we had together. Everything I let go. Worse, everything I pushed away. I know how much of an ass I was. I was afraid... I was confused... I- I'd never felt this way about anyone before..."

Ewan scoffed, and rolled his eyes. "Neither had I," he said. "But I knew damn well that if I did, I wouldn't treat them the way you treated me."

"I know," he said, "I know. And I'm sorry..."

"You were always sorry," said Ewan. "And you never changed. And maybe, you know, that's on me. That I kept letting you do that to me. Fooling me into thinking you would."

"I have changed," he pleaded. "I swear to you, I've changed. I'm here, aren't I?"

Ewan was about to open his mouth to speak, but then he paused.

He did have a point there...

He knew how much it must have taken him to come out here, to this place he'd made so vividly clear he hated so much.

"Not good enough," he said finally.

"You're here too," said Lance. "I mean, that's got to mean something- doesn't it?"

"It doesn't mean anything," said Ewan. "I thought I would meet you here instead of in the village and try to spare you some humiliation."

"Because you care about me," he said, and at the hardening of his face, he quickly amended, "Or maybe you don't. I don't know. But I have to believe that that's true. Even if it's just a very small part of you. And even if it's not true, I care so much about you Ewan. More than you could possibly-"

"No," said Ewan. "You care about yourself. If you cared about me, you wouldn't have come back here. Hell, if you cared about me, you wouldn't have let me go in the first place..."

"I'm sorry," he said, shaking his head again. "I'm sorry... If I have to spend the rest of my life saying it, I'm sorry..."

"I don't want you to spend the rest of your life saying it," said Ewan. "What I want is someone who doesn't need to spend of the rest of their life apologizing to me. Someone I can trust not to demolish my heart the way that you did. The way that you have a thousand times over. And you, Lance, are not that man."

His words were harsher than he intended them to be. He didn't want to push him away, or at least he didn't believe that he did. What he did want was penitence. To believe that what this man was telling him was true, and not just another display of crocodile tears. He'd seen these plenty of times before, after all, and the only place they'd led was to this very moment.

He'd already climbed so far from the place where he'd last fallen, and he wasn't about to be forced to start over again from scratch...

"What can I do?" Lance pleaded, his voice more heartbreaking than Ewan had ever heard it before. "What can I do to prove it to you? What can I do to make things right, to show you that I-"

"Just- just go," he said, shaking his head. "Just go, please. I can't do this tonight. I just can't. I have to get back to-" here he almost mentioned Colin's name, but stopped himself at the last minute. "I just can't do this right now." he amended. "Come back tomorrow night, if you feel like that's what you have to do. But not tonight."

"I-" Lance said, his eyes glistening in the moonlight. Then he nodded. "You're right. It's late. I'm sorry."

He sighed, annoyed at hearing the word again.

"Goodnight Lance," he said, and turned back in the direction of the village.

"Goodnight Ewan," he said, and he heard him say, as he stepped into the distance, "I love you. I've always loved you. And I always will."

He kept on walking.

Chapter 6

Slowly, very slowly, they rebuilt.

Night, after night, after night.

Lance continued to show up there in the woods, very much like clockwork, never missing a night.

This alone was impressive to him, knowing as he did how painful it must be for him to keep returning to this place. To keep reminding himself of the world he'd left behind.

He explained to Ewan during their visits what he already knew- that it had been this place that had made him behave the way he had toward him. The memories. The fears. The regrets.

It hadn't been Ewan. It had been entirely Lance.

He'd been too defensive. Too irrational. He'd refused to even discuss the issue with Ewan, afraid as he was of being tied down, consumed, and drawn back into that forgotten life, which he'd burned so desperately to escape for so very long before his departure.

Ewan supposed he understood, to some degree.

He conceded that, in many ways, he hadn't been exactly gracious about the matter.

He'd been able to see how much the issue of returning to this place got to Lance, and maybe he could have been a bit more sensitive to that fact. He just wish they could have talked about it, instead of immediately breaking into fights whenever the subject came up.

Lance understood that, and admitted freely that that was entirely his fault.

And from there, things slowly began to heal.

Ewan still wasn't ready to rush into anything too fast, but their conversations, at least, began to verge on normal again.

They talked about what they'd been up to in the time since they were apart. Lance told him about his jobs as a bouncer, some of the interesting stories he'd amassed in his time working the clubs. He didn't go into detail about his sex life since Ewan had departed, regretting as he did that there had even been a sex life during that period for him to go into detail about.

Ewan, meanwhile, talked about life among his former Streak. He told them of how his fellow shifters had taken him in without question, made sure his needs were met, and did everything in their power to make sure he felt included, as he'd wished for so long someone might do.

Lance seemed glad to know that he'd been taken care of, if begrudging of the fact that the men he'd left behind had been filling the niche in the life that he'd foolishly abandoned.

Still Ewan resisted any mention of their child, thinking he would bring up the subject when the time was right.

Deep down, he thought his reasons had something to do with wanting to make sure Lance truly wanted him before he presented him with the truth. Not wanting to trap him into a commitment, or into some life he didn't genuinely want with Ewan. He needed to make sure that the words being spoken were a true representation of how he really felt, and of the man he now was, before he felt comfortable divulging such a significant piece of information.

At the rate things were going, though, he had the strangest feeling that he wouldn't be waiting for that much longer...

They'd been sitting together one night, talking and laughing at the trunk of a tree.

Ewan couldn't even remember what had just been said, but it had created a kind of warm glow about the entire scene. They both felt a little bit drunk, enamored with one another and the entire world around them. Lance's arm was around him, his fingers softly brushing against the muscles of his shoulder.

"You don't know how bad I missed the touch of your skin," he said, his voice low, his warm breath blowing onto Ewan's neck, giving him goosebumps. "The taste of your lips... The weight of your body against mine..."

Ewan could feel his face getting red, and his masculinity stiffening up down below. He lifted up his legs to try and minimize the apparentness of it, then said back in a whisper, "I missed feeling your hands on me... Having you take me, and bend me to your will... I missed wrapping my lips around you, and having you inside me..."

He was trembling now, a little bit surprised at himself for having gone this far with things.

Maybe, he thought, it was a sign that he'd finally forgiven him...

Then, suddenly, he felt the warm press of Lance's hands against the sides of his body. He pulled him up into him, holding him close, and the two men locked eyes on one another, staring with such an intensity that they might never look away.

"Well," said Lance, "If we both missed one another so much... And we're both right here... I would say it's time for a bit of a reunion, wouldn't you?"

Ewan smiled, and thought he could feel his heart stop.

They kissed.

He'd forgotten how delectable the taste of his lips had been. Warm. Sweet. Salty.

He'd forgotten how much he loved the sliding of that tongue into his mouth, a gesture that always made him lightheaded.

He'd forgotten those hands, sliding along his spine, falling down toward his ass, making his cock rise up into the air as his arousal intensified.

Then, God, he felt Lance's hand wrapping around him. The tight enclosure of those perfect fingers, stroking every hot inch of his stiffening cock, squeezing out rivulets of pre-ejaculate as he pushed the skin from base to tip, his touch somehow simultaneously firm and silken and driving him absolutely mad.

He inhaled deep, he held his breath-

And then he pulled away.

Lance moved respectfully back, but looked hurt.

"God, I'm sorry," he said. "Was I- is this too fast, or?"

But Ewan shook his head, still trying to catch his breath.

"No... No, it's not that," he said, and thought for a long moment. He was afraid of what he needed to say to him, but knew that it had to be done. "I want you, so badly right now, it's just- I need to tell you something first..."

"Tell me," said Lance, seeming certain that nothing he had to say could possibly change how he felt.

He stared at him for a long moment, trying to think of some way to soften the blow.

In the end, though, he knew that his only real recourse was to come right out and say it.

"You made me pregnant," he finally confessed, "Right before I left you."

A stunned silence.

Lance stared at him, his eyes wide, and glistening softly in the darkness.

"I- you-" he muttered, like he could scarcely conceive of the notion. "Did you... Keep it?" he finally managed to get out.

"No, I- I mean yeah," Ewan was shaking his head, unable to make his words and body language align. "I had him a few months ago. A healthy baby boy. His name is Colin..."

"Colin," Lance repeated, seemingly at a distance. "I'm- I'm a father..."

Ewan nodded. "I'm- I'm sorry I didn't tell you earlier... I needed to know that-"

"That you could trust me," said Lance, like he was deeply ashamed of the fact.

"Well... Yes..." said Ewan. "And- can I? I mean... Is that something that you feel you're- that you're really ready for?"

Lance kept on looking off into space, then finally looked up at him with tears in his eyes.

"Are you kidding?" he asked, his blank expression suddenly peeling wide into a smile. "I think this might be the happiest moment of my entire life!"

They kissed again.

Lance wrapped his arms tight around Ewan's back, pulling him up into his chest.

Ewan craved the warmth of his body, the slow drawing of his damp flesh up along him.

More than anything, he glowed internally with a happiness that defied words. Knowing at last, after months of remaining in limbo, that the man he loved wanted the child they'd made together. That he was, in fact, thrilled by the news that he'd spent so very long keeping to himself.

He pressed his hands against Lance's own chest, his fingers dripping like liquid along the course of his musculature, running up and down along his body in a slow, steady circuit of movement.

He could feel Lance getting hard beneath him, his cock stiffening up between Ewan's own legs. Ewan wondered whether somehow this was an inappropriate response to the news he'd just shared, yet he found his own penis lengthening, pressing up against Lance's, and he decided they'd both be better off not to fight the impulse.

At last they pulled away from another, both breathing heavily, both staring wildly at one another as they prepared to pick right back up from where they'd left off earlier.

"I think maybe this calls for a bit of a celebration..." said Lance. "Don't you?"

Ewan smirked at him.

"I think it just might," he said.

He leaned back into him, and planted a soft kiss in the center of his alpha's chest.

He pulled back again, maintaining eye contact, and planted another, a few inches lower on his body.

And then, down, down, down, he went.

He opened his mouth wide, and bowed his head down into Lance's lap.

Lance moaned, and pressed his thighs up into him.

He wrapped his lips around every inch of that long, hard cock, pulling its heat up into that of his tightly sealed mouth. He rolled his tongue around every thick, delectable inch of it as he drew himself down, lapping him hungrily up, choking on him as he pushed him toward the back of his throat.

He'd honestly forgotten, in the time that they'd been apart, just what a difficult pill Lance had always been to swallow.

He had, however, always been a welcome one...

Lance held him by the nape of his neck once he was all the way down, and forced him to stay in place and gag on him, letting him savor the sensation of his throbbing cock as it pulsed with pleasure in his mouth. Then, slowly, he pressed his fingers along through Ewan's hair, and pulled him slowly back up along himself, dragging him all the way up to his tip.

Ewan's nostrils flared mightily, struggling to take in the air as his heart boomed in his chest.

Lance gave him a moment to recover, and then pushed him back down onto himself again, guiding his blowjob with a single hand, and controlling his movements with an almost unbearably sexy effortlessness.

Ewan choked, and strained, and felt tears streaming from his eyes as he sucked on the tumescent rod of his alpha, so happy to taste him again, to swallow the luscious streams of jizz that poured down his throat, to feel the controlling of hand of his bedroom master, pushing him to his limits, making him so very high with arousal that he didn't think he could ever climb back down again.

It went on for several glorious minutes, swallowing him up, spitting him back out again, then swallowing him up once more, coating him in a hot, syrupy sheath of his fluid, an ideal lubrication for what was to come.

At last, Lance pushed his face all the way down into himself and held it there, his muscles twitching as a clear indication that he was trying to hold back an orgasm. Then he let out a deep gasp, his body shivering as he pulled Ewan's face back along with him again, a long strand of spit dangling from his lips to the fully raised head of his penis.

"You really know how to please a man," said Lance, a lustful grin on his face.

Ewan smirked back at him, still trying to catch his breath.

"I was going to say the same thing about you..."

He put his hands on the sides of Lance's body, and lifted him up off of the ground onto his feet. He stood up behind him, and manhandled him around so that he was facing the tree. Ewan's placed his hands out flat against the bark and stood with his legs spread-eagled, placing himself fully on display for the taking.

He felt the vigorous clap of Lance's hands against his ass, sending a jolt of sensation up along his entire body. His penis leapt, and he felt himself go just a little bit dizzy as Lance came up behind him, sliding his wet cock up and down along his crack.

God, how he'd missed this subjugation, this total and complete surrender to the man he loved...

"I don't think I could possibly imagine a sweeter reunion..." Lance whispered into his ear.

Then spread apart the cheeks of his ass, slid the tip of his erection into Ewan's sphincter, and pushed himself inside.

Ewan felt as though he'd died and gone to heaven.

Lance slammed all the way down inside him, and instantly began to thrust into his body, not sparing him a moment's buildup as the instinct for domination overtook him. Ewan cried out passionately as he felt himself being taken, his head rocking as Lance slammed into him, his prostate burning, the endless crushing of his muscles feeling like it might be enough to crumple him into a tiny ball of nothingness beneath his weight.

"Oh yes! Oh God! Oh yes, please! Please, fuck me!" he begged, his body needing it as much as his soul after having gone without for more than a year's time.

He could tell, from Lance's fast, steady pumping, that he hadn't undergone any similar period of abstinence, but he found that he didn't really care all that much at that moment.

He was too grateful for his endurance to complain about anything in the world...

"God, you really want it, don't you?" said Lance, and he took a firm hold of his rear, and slammed up into him harder than ever.

Ewan cried out, and wished he had some way of focusing the hot wave of sensation now traveling from his ass, up through his balls and along the shaft of his cock.

As though reading his thoughts and perfectly intuiting his needs, Lance reached around and grabbed a firm handful of him, wrapping his fingers around him, pumping him like mad as he continued to slam him from behind.

It quickly became too much for him to take...

The vicious masturbation, coupled with the angry beating of his prostate, set off an explosion of sensation inside him, a euphoria he'd once known, long ago, and had spent the entire past year and a half or so merely fantasizing about.

He cried out at the top of his lungs, and Lance yanked the skin of his cock clear back, holding him wrapped tightly in his grip. Without a second's delay he began to cum all over the tree, bands of his white hot fluid shooting onto the bark and dripping down, or else blasting up against his own taut stomach, and all over Lance's trembling hand.

Finally the sensations died down, and he was left standing there in Lance's grip, wide-eyed, exhausted- but Lance was still far from finished with him.

In fact, now that Ewan's needs were satisfied, he was able to double down his focus on ramming him up the ass, slamming his pelvis forward at twice the speed, and fucking his tight hole to the point he grew raw. He grunted, and roared, and dug his nails into Ewan's skin, possessing him thoroughly, reducing him to an extension of himself, an instrument of his pleasure.

Ewan loved every violent moment of it, and could feel a fresh, improbable wave of euphoria building up inside him, so very shortly after the first had been exhausted.

At last, with a mighty, herculean force, he shoved every blessed inch of himself up into his omega's trembling body, nearly causing his legs to buckle from the weight, and from the sheer, explosive pleasure of it.

Lance let out his loudest, most deafening roar yet, a roar truly befitting his species, and came like a fountain inside Ewan's ass, packing him full to the brim with a flood of his hot, potent sperm. It rushed up inside him and coated the tight channel of his ass, spilling along the narrow tunnel in its thickness and abundance, rolling and dripping back out of him onto his buttocks, his balls, his quivering thighs. And yet it still kept coming and coming, the warm delectable bands setting off a massive fire in Ewan's deepest, most intimate depths.

It was all too much for him to take.

He yelled.

He screamed.

He tore bark from the tree as the second orgasm gripped him, tighter, hotter, more powerful than before.

It started in his pelvis, pulling in his ass, his nuts, his cock, and burning through every inch of them all. Then it burst outward, racing to impossible parts of his anatomy. Traveling along his thighs, all the way down to the tips of his toes. It rose up the trunk of his body, out along his arms, all the way to his fingers. It made the hairs on the back of his neck stand on end, and made his head feel as though it might begin to spin atop his neck, and go floating off into the sky.

Every inch of him was alight, on fire, absolutely consumed with pleasure in the racing moments that ensued.

And as Lance held him there, subjecting him to such glorious, indecent pleasure, refusing to relent until every last urge in his body had been satisfied, it hit him with full strength just how desperately he'd been missing all of this. How badly he needed it in his life, and how empty it had all seemed without it.

But now, at last, here it was again. Returned to him. Restored to him in fullness, at last.

And he wasn't about to let it go again...

EPILOGUE

"He- he's so beautiful," said Lance, his eyes wide, his lip trembling. Ewan had never seen this side of him before- he'd never even really suspected that it could exist.

Lance ran one mighty hand over the dome of Colin's soft, round head, stroking the faint brown hair, and Ewan felt a shiver of sensation pass through his body, which had very little to do with what the two men had just gotten through doing to one another in the woods...

"You can hold him," he encouraged.

"Are you sure?" Lance asked, looking worried. "I mean I don't want to wake him up..."

"It's okay," he said. "He's always been a pretty sound sleeper..."

Very carefully, Lance swept the child up into his mighty arms, and held him against his strong, bare chest. It was another one of those heartbreaking moments that Ewan had known so many of ever since Colin's birth, and it was made all the more potent by the light whimper from the child's mouth as he cradled him in his arms.

"God, I love you," said Ewan, and Lance looked up at him, and smiled.

"I'm so sorry," he said. "That I wasn't here for you... For both of you..."

Ewan shook his head.

"No more sorries," he said. "The past is gone now. We're together again, and what matters is that the three of us move forward. That we stay together again, no matter what."

"You're right," said Lance, and Ewan loved the little drunk smile across his face as he stared down at his child.

After a moment, Colin began to cry, and a look of panic crossed over Lance's face as he tried to calm him down.

"Sh-sh-sh," he hissed, softly rocking him, to very little avail.

"Here," said Ewan, holding out his hands. He took the child, pulled him to his chest, and made short work of calming him back down again.

"What the hell did you do?" asked Lance, and Ewan just smiled at him.

Then he sighed, thinking the matter now at hand was going to be an unpleasant one to discuss.

"Listen," he said. "If the three of us are going to be together, I don't really think we can stay here..."

Lance frowned, considering this.

"But I- I don't understand... You love this place," he said. "The whole reason you left was so that you could be somewhere you belonged. Somewhere that- well, I guess I know now- where our child belongs."

"I don't belong here," he said resignedly, shaking his head. "You were right about that much. I belong where you are. Where our son is."

He looked sadly at him, and shook his head.

"I'm willing to be here. To return here with you. You're right that the three of us belong together, and it's wrong of me to take you and Colin to live in a world where you don't belong. I see that now."

"It's not that," said Ewan, looking a little bit sad. "It's... Well... I know you were always a little bit hesitant about coming back to this place. But after hearing Ulric and the other shifters talk about you the way that they do. Well... I'm not totally sure you can come back here. I'm not sure whether you would even live to tell the tale, even if you tried. A lot of them- they see you as a traitor. As having abandoned your life with them, and running off to live among the humans..."

"Oh," said Lance, rather stunned by this, as though just having considered it for the very first time. "I- I guess I see that now," he said, and shook his head. "God... I really screwed everything up for you didn't I?" He held his head in his hands, looking ashamed. "I was so selfish, from the beginning. Thinking I deserved better than everyone else. Thinking I was missing something, when I had the entire world right there at my feet..."

Ewan could see how much this was distressing him, and he reached out to place a hand on his wrist, hoping it might calm him down.

"You left," he said calmly, "Believing that there was a better life for you out there somewhere. And that the only way you could ever find it was by putting the past behind you, and finding somewhere you truly belonged in the world. It's the exact same reason I left, and abandoned you the way that I did. I realize that now. But, in the end, I think the important thing is that we both found each other... And as long as we're together, I don't think it matters whether Colin is raised among humans or among shifters. All that matters is that he has two caring fathers who love him with all their heart, and who love one another just as much. That's all I really want for him, and for us. That's all I ever really could want. For us to be together..."

Lance took a deep breath, then nodded, as though finally convinced that he was telling the truth.

"Okay," he said. "Okay..."

He reached out for him, and laced his fingers tightly through those of Ewan's free hand.

"I love you," he said, "So much. With every ounce of my heart. Every single fiber of my being."

"I know you do," said Ewan. "That's why I can't wait for us to start over again, and finally begin the rest of our lives together..."

The two men leaned into one another and kissed, slowly, passionately, their beating hearts softly strobing against the small, warm body of the child they'd produced together in their love.

———

Two fully grown tigers crept through the shadows, moving silently along beneath the cover of the forest. One of them held a small, sleepy cub in its teeth, carrying it along by the scruff of its neck. Aside from this little miracle, they carried absolutely nothing whatsoever on their person.

Nor did they know, exactly, just where it was that they intended on going once they made it to the edge of the forest.

Whether back to the city, off to some other, more secluded section of woodland, or any number of a million other possible destinations.

All they really knew was that the three of them were together, and that as long as that was the case, wherever they ended up in the end could truly be called home.

*****

Don't miss out!

Visit the website below and you can sign up to receive emails whenever Van Cole publishes a new book. There's no charge and no obligation.

https://books2read.com/r/B-A-RTRV-JNQIC

BOOKS 2 READ

Connecting independent readers to independent writers.

Also by Van Cole

3 Man Huddle: MMM Best Friend Romance
His Alpha Wolf: Gay First Time Romance
A Dragon's Miracle: Gay Dragon MPREG Romance
Double-Teamed: MMM First Time Football Romance
His Football Star: Gay Second Chance Romance
Love In My Town: MM First Time Romance
Training A Hockey Star
Game Night
Double Shift
Take A Shot
Dear Professor
Getting Inked
Ninth Inning
Triple Threat
Seducing My Best Friend's Brother
My Protector
The Blueprint
Show Me The Way
End Zone
Matched To His Tiger
Love At First Puck
My Straight Boss
Falling For The Alpha
My Boss
On Thin Ice